P9-AGT-691

# RICHARD SCARRY'S
## Great Big Schoolhouse
### Readers

# One, Two, AH-CHOO!

Illustrated by Huck Scarry
Written by Erica Farber

## STERLING CHILDREN'S BOOKS
New York

Sally Cat had a cold.
One, two, AH-CHOO!

Huckle played games with her.
Lowly played games with her.

Wow! Look at all the toys!

Mrs. Cat had a cold.

One, two, AH-CHOO!

Lowly made toast for her.

Huckle got juice for her.

OOPS! The tray fell.

The boys fell.

One, two, AH-CHOO!

Mr. Cat sneezed.

Oh, no! No more tissues!

Huckle and Lowly went to
the store. There was Ella.
One, two, AH-CHOO!
Ella sneezed.
She dropped an orange.

Huckle picked up the orange.
CRASH! There went the oranges!

When they got home,
there was Bridget.
One, two, AH-CHOO!
Bridget sneezed.

"Here is a tissue," said Huckle.

He did not see the wheelbarrow.
OOPS!

It was time for school.

Huckle and Lowly ran for the bus.

One, two, AH-CHOO!

Arthur sneezed.

He dropped his backpack.

His stuff fell out.

Huckle and Lowly picked up
his stuff.

"I have a cold," said Arthur.

"I am going home."

At school, Molly sneezed.
One, two, AH-CHOO!

She sneezed again.
One, two, AH-CHOO!

So, Huckle and Lowly took
Molly to the nurse.

One, two, AH-CHOO!

Frances sneezed.

Frances had a cold, too.

So, Huckle and Lowly took Frances
to the nurse.

14

Huckle, Lowly, and Skip played tag.

One, two, AH-CHOO! Skip sneezed.

Skip had a cold.

He took himself to the nurse.

Huckle and Lowly looked at Miss Honey. They were the only ones left at school.

So, Huckle and Lowly made get-well cards.

One, two, AH-CHOO!
Miss Honey sneezed.
Huckle and Lowly made her
a get-well card, too.

Huckle and Lowly took a
get-well card to Ella.

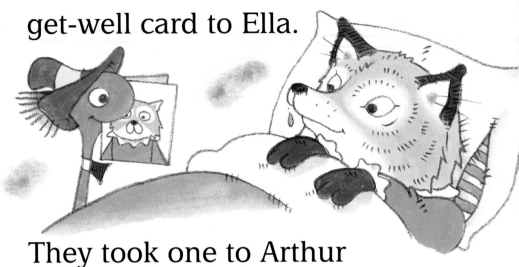

They took one to Arthur
and one to Molly.

They took one to Frances…

…one to Skip…

…and one to Bridget.

Thank you, Huckle and Lowly!

Then Huckle and Lowly went home. One, two, AH-CHOO! Huckle and Lowly sneezed.

Huckle and Lowly had colds, too.

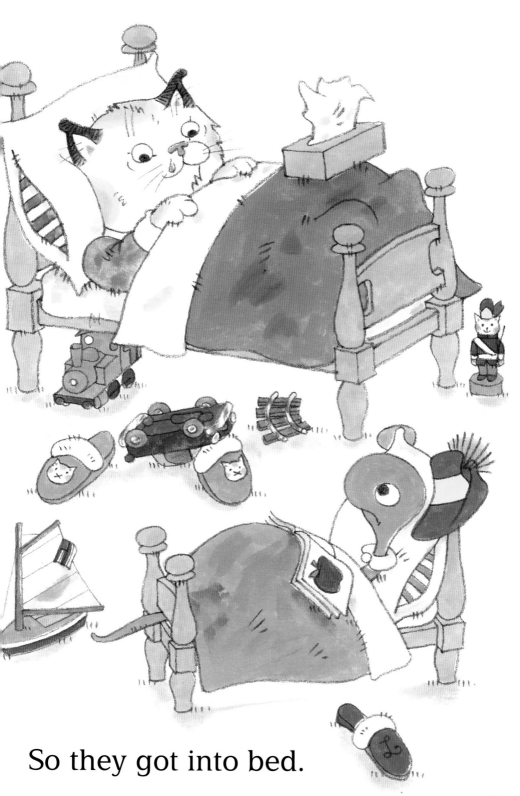

So they got into bed.

Sally played games with them.
Mrs. Cat got toast and juice
for them.

Mr. Cat got tissues for them.
One, two, AH-CHOO!

## STERLING CHILDREN'S BOOKS
New York

An Imprint of Sterling Publishing
387 Park Avenue South
New York, NY 10016

ISBN 978-1-4549-0380-2 (hardcover)
ISBN 978-1-4549-0381-9 (paperback)

Produced by

JR Sansevere

Distributed in Canada by Sterling Publishing
c/o Canadian Manda Group, 165 Dufferin Street
Toronto, Ontario, Canada M6K 3H6
Distributed in the United Kingdom by GMC Distribution Services
Castle Place, 166 High Street, Lewes, East Sussex, England BN7 1XU
Distributed in Australia by Capricorn Link (Australia) Pty. Ltd.
P.O. Box 704, Windsor, NSW 2756, Australia

For information about custom editions, special sales, premium and corporate purchases,
please contact Sterling Special Sales at 800-805-5489 or specialsales@sterlingpublishing.com.

Printed in China

Lot #:
2 4 6 8 10 9 7 5 3 1
11/13

www.sterlingpublishing.com/kids